MASSACHUSETTS

in words and pictures

BY DENNIS B. FRADIN

ILLUSTRATIONS BY RICHARD WAHL

MAPS BY LEN W. MEENTS

Consultant:
Albert H. Whitaker, Jr.
Archivist of the Commonwealth
Boston

 CHILDRENS PRESS, CHICAGO

For my mother, Selma Brindel Fradin, with love

For their help, the author thanks:

Dr. Albert H. Whitaker, Jr., Archivist of the Commonwealth

Dr. Dena F. Dincauze, Associate Professor of Anthropology, University of Massachusetts at Amherst

The Old North Bridge at Concord, where a troop of Minutemen stopped the British at the beginning of the American Revolutionary War

Library of Congress Cataloging in Publication Data

Fradin, Dennis B
    Massachusetts in words and pictures.

    SUMMARY: Discusses the history, geography, famous citizens, places of interest, and industry of the "Bay State."
    1. Massachusetts—Juvenile literature. [1. Massachusetts] I. Wahl, Richard, 1939- II. Meents, Len W. III. Title.
F64.3.F7   974.4   80-26161
ISBN 0-516-03921-0

Picture Acknowledgments:

H. FLINT RANNEY, NANTUCKET: Cover, page 15

DIVISION OF TOURISM, MASSACHUSETTS DEPARMENT OF COMMERCE AND DEVELOPMENT: pages 2, 9 (bottom right), 18, 29, 35

CAPE COD CHAMBER OF COMMERCE: pages 5, 39, 40

PLYMOUTH COUNTY DEVELOPMENT COUNCIL: pages 9 (left and top right), 11, 12, 32 (right), 36 (top)

PIONEER VALLEY ASSOCIATION, NORTHAMPTON: pages 13, 25, 32 (left), 33, 34

AMERICAN AIRLINES: page 17 (right)

OLD NORTH CHURCH, BOSTON: page 17 (left)

MASSACHUSETTS HISTORICAL SOCIETY: page 20

TWA: page 26

UNITED AIR LINES, INC.: page 27

BASKETBALL HALL OF FAME: page 31

THE WITCH HOUSE, SALEM: page 36 (bottom)

COVER: The sailing schooner *Bill of Rights* entering Nantucket Harbor

Massachusetts (mass • ah • CHOO • setz) is a state in the northeastern United States. It was named for the Massachusett Indian tribe. The word *Massachusett* is thought to mean "the place of the great hill."

Many important events in United States history took place in Massachusetts. The Pilgrims arrived there in 1620. The Revolutionary War (rev • oh • LOO • shun • airy wore) started in Massachusetts. The state was the birthplace of three presidents. They were John Adams, John Quincy (KWIN • see) Adams, and John F. Kennedy.

Do you know where our first Thanksgiving was held? Or where the first public school and library in the United

States were formed? Do you know where Paul Revere (PAWL ree • VEER) made his famous horseback ride? Or where the telephone was invented?

You have probably guessed the answer to all these questions: Massachusetts!

Over 100 million years ago dinosaurs (DINE • ah • sores) roamed through Massachusetts. This was long before there were any people on Earth. The last dinosaurs died long ago. But their huge footprints have been found in Massachusetts.

Over a million years ago the Ice Age began. Mountains of ice—called *glaciers* (GLAY • sherz)—moved down from the north. All of Massachusetts was covered by the ice. The glaciers did much to shape the land. They deepened valleys. The valleys later filled with water. They became lakes. Look at a map of Massachusetts. You will see a piece of land shaped like a fishhook. It is called Cape Cod. Cape Cod was formed by rock, sand, and gravel that were carried into the ocean by glaciers.

These Indian tools, pipes, pieces of pottery, and arrowheads were found in Massachusetts.

People first came to Massachusetts at least 10,000 years ago. Stone spearheads, knives, and tools of ancient people have been found. The ancient people hunted large animals. They learned to fish and gather plant foods. Over 1,000 years ago, they learned to farm.

In more recent times, a number of Indian tribes lived in Massachusetts. The Massachusett Indians were just one of these tribes. The Pocumtuc (poh • KUHM • tuhk), Wampanoag (wahm • pah • NO • ag), Nauset (NAW • siht), and Nipmuc (NIHP • muhk) were four others.

5

The Indians gathered clams and oysters. They grew corn, beans, squash, and pumpkins. They hunted deer and birds in the forests.

The Indians lived in long houses. They were made of tree limbs and bark. They built canoes for traveling on rivers. They used beads, called *wampum* (WAHM • puhm), for money. Wooden bowls, clothing, and arrows made by the Indians can be seen in Massachusetts museums today. But there are only about 5,000 Indian people in Massachusetts now.

It is not known who the first explorers in Massachusetts were. Some think that in about the year 1000 Leif Ericson (LEEF AIR • ick • sun) and some Norsemen (men from Norway) explored Massachusetts. In the 1400s French and Spanish fishermen may have fished in Massachusetts waters. In 1498 John Cabot (KAB • uht) might have explored Massachusetts for England.

Bartholomew Gosnold (bahr • THAHL • uh • myoo GAHZ • nohld) explored Massachusetts for England in 1602. He caught codfish in a place he named *Cape Cod*. He named an island *Martha's Vineyard* (MAHR • thuhz VIHN • yerd) after his daughter. The English had explored Massachusetts. So England claimed Massachusetts.

The Pilgrims were a religious (ree • LIH • juhs) group. They lived in England in the early 1600s. They were not allowed to follow their religion. They looked for a place where they would be free to worship as they pleased. First they went to Holland (HAHL • luhnd). Then they heard about a land called America. They decided to form a colony there. They were sure they would have religious freedom in America.

The Pilgrims went to Plymouth (PLIH • muhth), England. There they boarded a ship called the *Mayflower*. On September 16, 1620, the Pilgrims left England. They headed for America. From the moment they left England, everything the Pilgrims did became a famous part of American history.

Storms hit the *Mayflower* as it crossed the ocean. The ship started to leak. Repairs were made. After 66 days at sea, the *Mayflower* reached Massachusetts.

The Pilgrims explored the coast. Then, on December 21, 1620, they chose a place to settle. They named it *Plymouth*. There was a rock nearby that came to be known as *Plymouth Rock*.

The *Mayflower II* (left), a replica
of the original *Mayflower*, is
anchored at Plymouth.
Plymouth Rock (above) is now protected
by a granite monument (above top).

Before they got off the ship, the Pilgrims formed their
own government. The agreement they made was called
the *Mayflower Compact*. It was one of the first plans of
government in what is now the United States.

The Pilgrims built wooden houses at Plymouth. Soon they had a settlement. The Plymouth Colony was the second permanent English settlement in what is now the United States. Jamestown, Virginia, had been the first.

Life was very hard for the Pilgrims during the winter of 1620. They shot some wild animals for food. But much of the time they were hungry and cold. In that first winter, about half of the Pilgrims died.

The Pilgrims must have wondered if any of them would survive. But in the spring, help came from the Indians. Massasoit (MASS • uh • saw • iht) was the chief of the Wampanoag tribe. He made a treaty with the Pilgrims. He said that his people would live in peace with

Plimouth Plantation, shown in these pictures, is a re-creation of the original Plymouth village.

them. Squanto and other Indians taught the Pilgrims how to plant corn. The Indians also showed them where to fish and hunt.

The Pilgrims had a good harvest in the fall of 1621. They decided to celebrate. They invited Massasoit and other Indians to a feast. The Pilgrims thanked God that they had survived. They ate turkey and geese, oysters and lobsters. There were also races and games at the three-day party. This was the first Thanksgiving. When you have your Thanksgiving dinner this November, remember the Pilgrims who held our first Thanksgiving in 1621. Remember, too, the Indians who helped the Pilgrims survive.

In 1627 another religious group came to Massachusetts. They were the Puritans (PYOOR • ih • tehnz). They formed what was called the Massachusetts Bay Colony. John Winthrop (WIN • thruhp) was their leader. The Puritans founded the town of Boston (BAW • stun) in 1630.

At first the settlers in Massachusetts farmed and hunted like the Indians. Then some became schoolteachers and doctors. Towns grew bigger. More

The Jenney Grist Mill, built in 1636 in Plymouth, has been reconstructed and continues to grind grain daily, just as it did then.

This memorial in Deerfield honors the settlers who were killed in the Bloody Brook Massacre during King Philip's War.

towns were built. By 1640 about 16,000 settlers lived in Massachusetts.

As time passed, the Indians saw that the settlers were taking their lands. Chief Massasoit had lived in peace with the Pilgrims. His son, King Philip (FILL • ihp), became chief in 1662. King Philip was afraid the settlers would take all the Indian land. He decided to drive the settlers out. He led the Indians in what is called "King Philip's War." Many Indians and settlers were killed in the fighting. King Philip's war was lost in 1678.

During the 1600s, there were many "firsts" in Massachusetts. In 1635 the Boston Latin School was founded. It was the first public school in what is now the United States. In 1636 Harvard (HAHR • verd) College was founded. It was the first college in our country. In 1638 America's first library was formed, at Harvard. In 1690 the first newspaper in America was printed at Boston.

In 1691 the Plymouth Colony and the Massachusetts Bay Colony joined. They formed one Massachusetts colony. It was ruled by governors from England. The colony didn't have the good farmland that could be found in other areas. So in the 1700s many Massachusetts people turned to the sea to make their living. Ships from Nantucket (nan • TUHK • eht) and New Bedford (NOO BED • ferd) went out after whales. The whale oil was used to light lamps. Cod and other fish were caught by Massachusetts fishermen.

Shipbuilding also became a big business. Cloth, shoes, and guns were other Massachusetts products of the 1700s.

From 1754 to 1763 England fought a war with France in America. This was called the French and Indian War. Wars cost money. To help pay for the war, England made the American colonists pay big taxes. Tea and other products brought from England were taxed.

The colonists didn't want to pay these taxes. Besides, many didn't think of themselves as English people any longer. They had built towns and farms in America. They

Nantucket (below) was an important whaling town in the 1700s and 1800s.

thought of themselves as Americans. People spoke of forming their own country. They knew they would have to fight a war with England to do it. Some of the main events leading to the Revolutionary War took place in Massachusetts.

In 1770 angry people gathered in Boston. They attacked an English soldier. English soldiers fired their guns into the crowd. Five Americans were killed. This famous event was called the Boston Massacre (MASS • ih • kuhr). It put the Americans in a fighting mood.

In 1773 three English ships loaded with tea sat in Boston Harbor. Americans dressed up as Indians. They took the tea off the ships. They dumped it into the bay. This famous event is called the Boston Tea Party. It brought England and the American colonies even closer to war.

Revolutionary War fighting began in 1775. It started in Massachusetts. In April, English soldiers headed toward the town of Lexington (LEKS • ing • tun), Massachusetts. American soldiers known as

Above: Lexington Common, where the Revolutionary War began.

Left: *The Midnight Ride of Paul Revere,* by W.R. Leigh, shows Revere riding to Lexington to warn the Americans that the British were coming.

"minutemen" lived in the area. They were called that because they could get ready to fight in a minute.

Paul Revere rode on horseback from Boston to Lexington. He warned the Americans that the English were coming. At dawn on April 19, the English soldiers met the American minutemen. "Stand your ground," the American leader John Parker told his men. "Don't fire unless fired upon. But if they mean to have war, let it begin here." The Revolutionary War *did* begin right there at Lexington. The Americans were outnumbered.

Eight of their men were killed. On that same day the English marched to nearby Concord (KAHN • kerd). Americans had stored supplies there. Minutemen and English soldiers fought at North Bridge, near Concord. Three English soldiers and two Americans were killed in this fight.

Few people died at Lexington and Concord. But these battles are famous because they were the first of the Revolutionary War.

In June of 1775 the English beat the Americans in the Battle of Bunker Hill, near Boston. The next month, on

The Battle of Bunker Hill

July 3, 1775, George Washington took command of the American army at Cambridge (KAYM • brihj). In March of 1776 Americans finally drove the English out of Boston. This was one of the first American victories in the war.

About 88,000 Massachusetts men helped George Washington win other battles. By 1783 the Americans had won the Revolutionary War. A new country — the United States of America — had been born!

Massachusetts became our sixth state on February 6, 1788. Boston was the capital. Massachusetts was nicknamed the *Bay State*. This was because the Puritans had settled in the area of Massachusetts Bay. Their group was known as the Massachusetts Bay Colony.

The new state soon produced two presidents. John Adams was born in what is now Quincy, Massachusetts, in 1735. He went to Harvard. He became a lawyer. Adams was a leader during the Revolutionary War. But when the war ended he helped make the peace treaty with England. From 1789 to 1797 Adams served as the

Abigail and John Adams, painted by Benjamin Blythe.

first vice president of the United States. From 1797 to 1808 John Adams served as our country's second president. During troubled times, John Adams helped keep peace with other countries. He died on the Fourth of July in 1826. He was almost 91 years old.

John Quincy Adams (1767-1848) was John Adams' son. He was born in Quincy, too. John Quincy Adams traveled around the world with his father. He learned about world problems. John Quincy Adams was elected senator from Massachusetts in 1803. In 1825 he was elected the sixth president of the United States. John Adams and John Quincy Adams are the only father and son who were both presidents.

While the Adams men were working as presidents, much was happening in their home state. In the 1800s many factories were built in Massachusetts. The making of textiles (cloth) became important.

In the southern part of the United States, however, farming was the main way of making a living. Black slaves did the work on the farms. In the 1800s, Americans argued about slavery. William Lloyd Garrison, born in Newburyport (NOO • berry • pohrt), Massachusetts, hated slavery. He started a newspaper in Boston to help end slavery. It was called *The Liberator.* Some Massachusetts people helped slaves escape from the South all the way to Canada. The system of helping slaves escape was called the *underground railroad.*

Northerners and Southerners argued slavery for many years. They argued about taxes and other matters. The talking ended. Fighting began in 1861. This was the start of the Civil War. Massachusetts sent more than 160,000 men to fight on the Northern side. Massachusetts supplied ships for the North, too. By 1865 the North had won the Civil War.

Shortly after the Civil War ended, a man named Alexander Graham Bell came to Boston. He taught deaf people. Bell believed he could send the human voice over long distances. In 1876 he built a machine to do it. This was the telephone.

Other inventions have been made in the Bay State. The modern sewing machine was invented there. Many machines for speeding up factory work have been made in Massachusetts.

A very famous American was born in Brookline, Massachusetts, in 1917. His name was John Fitzgerald Kennedy. During World War II, Kennedy was commander of a boat. It was cut in two by an enemy ship. Pulling an injured man with him, Kennedy swam to an island. A few days later he and his men were rescued. In 1952 John F. Kennedy was elected United States

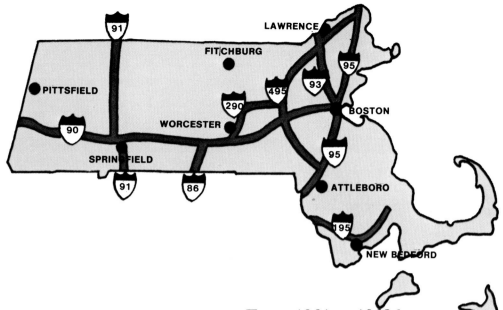

senator from Massachusetts. From 1961 to 1963 he

served as the thirty-fifth president. He was the youngest

man ever elected president. In 1963, Kennedy was shot

and killed while on a trip.

Much of the story of Massachusetts in the 1900s

involves manufacturing (making things in factories).

People have come from around the world to work in the

state's factories. Hundreds of products are now made in

Massachusetts. Many kinds of machines are made there.

Computers (kum • PYOO • terz) are made. Television parts

are made in the state. Shoes, clothes, bicycles,

schoolbooks, and foods are a few of the state's other

products. Today, Massachusetts is a leading

manufacturing state.

You have learned about some of Massachusetts' history. Now it is time for a trip—in words and pictures—through the Bay State.

Only five states are smaller than Massachusetts. From east to west its widest distance is 190 miles. From north to south its greatest distance is only 110 miles. But many beautiful and historic (hiss • TORE • ihk) places are packed into this small state!

Pretend you are in an airplane high above Massachusetts. Below, you can see many kinds of scenery. In the west you see the Berkshire (BURK • shur) Hills. You see the Taconic (tuh • KAHN • ihk) Mountains. Throughout the state you see blue lakes and rivers. The Connecticut (kuh • NET • ih • kut) is Massachusetts' main river. It flows south through the whole state. Do you see that huge body of water to the east of Massachusetts? That is the Atlantic Ocean.

Your airplane is landing in a city that lies near the Atlantic Ocean. This is Boston. Long ago, Massachusett

Indians lived in this area. In 1630 a group of Puritans led by John Winthrop founded Boston. Today, Boston is the biggest city in Massachusetts. It is also the capital of the state.

Take the Freedom Trail in Boston. This "trail" is a red line on the sidewalks of the city that will lead you to old houses and other historic places.

You will enjoy Faneuil (FAN • yoo • ell) Hall, built in 1742. This building was nicknamed the "Cradle of Liberty" by President John Adams. Many meetings to

The oxbow (bend) of the Connecticut River

The skyline of Boston as seen from the Charles River

protest English rule were held here in the 1700s. Nearby is the Boston Massacre site. This was where English soldiers killed five colonists. One of the Americans killed was Crispus Attucks (KRISP • us AT • uhks). He is thought to have been a runaway slave.

Visit the Boston Tea Party Ship and Museum (myoo • ZEE • uhm) in Boston Harbor. There you can learn about events that helped bring on the Revolutionary War.

You will enjoy the Paul Revere House. It was built in about 1680. It is the oldest building in downtown Boston.

This statue of Paul Revere is in Boston. The Old North Church can be seen in the background.

Paul Revere did more than make a famous ride. He was a silversmith. He made bells, cannons, and silverware of silver and other metals. He made the state seal. It is still used in Massachusetts. He was also the father of 16 children!

Visit the King's Chapel in downtown Boston. It was built in 1750. The king and queen of England gave objects to decorate this church. After the Revolutionary War, King's Chapel became the first Unitarian (yoo • nih • TARE • ee • uhn) church in our country. The large bell in the church was made by Paul Revere. "The sweetest bell we ever made," Revere wrote on it.

Do you see that big building with a golden dome? That is the State House. Lawmakers from all over Massachusetts meet there. You can watch them work on laws for the Bay State. In recent years, they have worked on laws to clean up the state's rivers and lakes. They have worked on laws to protect wildlife. They have worked on laws to help the elderly.

Boston has some great museums. At the Museum of Fine Arts you can see artworks from many countries. At the Museum of Science you can learn about dinosaurs, space ships, and stars. At the Boston Children's Museum you can learn about New England Indians and modern cities.

If you like music, listen to the Boston Symphony Orchestra (SIM • foe • nee OHR • kess • trah) or the Boston "Pops" Orchestra. If you like to be outdoors, go to the Boston Common. It is a famous old park. Long ago, it was a meadow where cows grazed!

This bronze statue of John Harvard stands in Harvard University Yard.

Boston people like sports. The Boston Red Sox slam the baseball around Fenway Park. The Bruins (BROO • ihnz) are the city's hockey team. The Celtics (SELL • tihks) are Boston's basketball team. A long, famous footrace is held in Boston. It is called the Boston Marathon. The New England Patriots (PAY • tree • uhtz) play football nearby, in Foxboro (FAHKS • burr • oh).

There are some interesting cities and towns near Boston. Visit Cambridge. The famous Harvard University (yoo • nih • VUHR • sih • tee) is in Cambridge.

Radcliffe College, Lesley College, and the Massachusetts Institute of Technology (tehk • NAHL • uh • jee) are also there. Cambridge has so many schools of higher learning that it is nicknamed *University City*.

Lexington and Concord are both near Boston. At these towns you can see where the first Revolutionary War battles were fought. Concord has another claim to fame. The tasty Concord grape was first grown there!

Head to Worcester (WOOS • tuhr). It is about 45 miles west of Boston. Nipmuc Indians once lived here. Settlers came in the late 1600s. Today, Worcester is one of the state's largest cities.

You will enjoy the Worcester Art Museum. There you can see artworks from many places and times.

A lot of tools and machinery are made in Worcester. Many other iron and steel products come from the city.

Head about 50 miles southwest of Worcester. You will come to the city of Springfield. Springfield lies on the Connecticut River. Settlers first entered the area in 1636.

In 1891, a Springfield teacher named James A. Naismith (NAY • smith) made up a new game. He put up some peach baskets at both ends of a gym. The idea was to throw the ball into the baskets. This was the beginning of basketball! The Springfield rifle (RYE • fehl) was also first made in Springfield.

Today, many kinds of machines are made in Springfield. Chemicals (KEHM • ih • kulz) and clothes are also made in the city.

James A. Naismith invented the game of basketball.

Farms such as this one (above) can be found throughout the Massachusetts countryside. Cranberries are big business in the state. The picture at right shows cranberries being harvested.

You have seen some of the state's biggest cities. Now let's travel through the Massachusetts countryside. You will see farms in many areas. Have you noticed all the cows? Milk is one of the state's leading farm products.

You could eat very well on Massachusetts farm products! Sweet corn, asparagus (ahs • PARE • ah • guss), potatoes, and cucumbers (KYOO • kuhm • buhrz) are grown by farmers. Tomatoes and strawberries are grown in Massachusetts. There's a good chance that the cranberries you ate with Thanksgiving dinner came from

Massachusetts. Almost half the country's cranberries come from the Bay State. Eggs are another Massachusetts farm product. Beef cattle, turkeys, and hogs are some of the livestock raised in the state.

The small towns in Massachusetts are quieter than the big cities. They are pretty, too. You will see old churches, schools, inns, and taverns. You will see covered bridges.

Historic buildings can be seen throughout the state. The Wells-Thorn House of Deerfield (below) and Williamsburg Church (left) are both in Pioneer Valley.

Head into the Berkshire Hills. They are in western
Massachusetts. People ski and hike in the Berkshires.
Mount Greylock is in the Berkshires, near the northwest
corner of the state. It rises 3,491 feet above sea level.
Mount Greylock is the state's highest point. At the
western edge of Massachusetts you will come to the
Taconic Mountains.

Forests cover many areas of Massachusetts. You will
see pine, oak, and maple trees in the state. In all, about
two-thirds of Massachusetts is forested. Paper and paper
products are made from some of the trees. The paper
that United States money is printed on is made in
Massachusetts.

Making maple sugar is
one of the major farm
industries in Pioneer
Valley in western
Massachusetts. This
picture shows maple
sap being collected.

The *Fishermen's Memorial* in Gloucester

You can see many animals in the forests. You might see deer and foxes. You can watch beavers building their dams on rivers. Porcupines (PORE • kyu • pynz) and skunks can be found. Pheasants (FEHZ • uhntz), ducks, and geese can also be seen flying through Massachusetts.

Head back to the northeast corner of Massachusetts. Go down the coast, along the Atlantic Ocean.

Gloucester (GLAH • stuhr) is in northeastern Massachusetts. Gloucester is a famous old fishing city. There is a statue in Gloucester called the *Fishermen's Memorial*. It is a reminder of the many Gloucester fishermen who died at sea.

At Plimouth Plantation, daily life is carried on just the way it was when the original settlers lived there. Farming, fishing, preparing food, building homes (above), and other activities are carried on throughout the year.
The Witch House in Salem (below) was the home of one of the judges at the witch trials.

Continue down the coast. You will see other towns that have fishing fleets. Massachusetts is a leading fishing state. Scallops, cod, shrimp, lobster, tuna, and swordfish are some of the seafoods brought back by Massachusetts fishermen. Much of the seafood is packaged right in Massachusetts.

Just a few miles southwest of Gloucester you will come to Salem (SAY • lehm). In the 1690s, people in Salem believed that some of the townspeople were witches. Trials were held. Nineteen people accused of being witches were hanged. You can visit the Witch House in Salem. It was a home of one of the judges at the witch trials.

What happened in Salem was one of the sad events in American history. In southeast Massachusetts visit Plymouth. Here some of our greatest events took place. This was where the Pilgrims landed in 1620. Visit Plimoth Plantation. It has been built to look like the Pilgrims' village. You can climb aboard the *Mayflower*

II. It has been built to look like the original *Mayflower.*

Would you like to see a house where Pilgrims lived? Very near Plymouth visit the John and Priscilla Alden (prih • SIHL • ah ALL • duhn) House. It is at Duxbury (DUHKS • bare • ee). It was built in about 1653. John Alden was one of the Pilgrims' leaders.

Visit the city of New Bedford. It is in southeast Massachusetts. Once it was a great whaling center. Today New Bedford is the leading fishing city in Massachusetts. It is one of the leading fishing cities in all of the eastern United States.

Finish your Massachusetts trip by going to Cape Cod. It is a piece of land that juts out into the Atlantic Ocean. Three sides of Cape Cod are touched by water. So it is a *peninsula* (peh • NIHN • suh • luh).

Cape Cod is an important vacation area. People enjoy its beaches and sand dunes. They visit Provincetown (PRAHV • ihnss • toun) and other old towns on Cape Cod.

The old coastal communities of
Cape Cod peninsula and the islands
of Nantucket and Martha's Vineyard
are important vacation areas.
These pictures show the tip of the
cape (top left), Provincetown (left),
and Sandy Neck Beach at Sandwich (above).

An artist at work
in Provincetown

Artists go to Cape Cod to paint pictures of the sea. You
can take boats from Cape Cod to islands such as
Martha's Vineyard and Nantucket. These islands are
also part of Massachusetts.

Places can't tell the whole story of Massachusetts.
This small state has produced a huge number of famous
and interesting people.

Benjamin Franklin (1706-1790) was born in Boston.
When Benjamin Franklin was seventeen years old, he
ran away to Philadelphia (fill • ah • DELL • fee • yah). Just
about whatever you can think of, Franklin could do. He
printed books. He invented a heating stove. Once, he flew
a kite during a storm. He proved that lightning is
electricity. Franklin was also a famous American

statesman. He signed the Declaration of Independence. He also signed the Constitution of the United States.

John Hancock (1737-1793) was born in Braintree, Massachusetts. He was the first person to sign the Declaration of Independence. Hancock was an American leader during the Revolutionary War.

Henry David Thoreau (thuh • ROH) (1817-1862) was born in Concord. He became a great writer.

Massachusetts has produced many other great writers. Ralph Waldo Emerson, Emily Dickinson, Amy Lowell, and Nathaniel Hawthorne are just three of them. The famous children's writer, Dr. Seuss, was born there, too!

Clara Barton (1821-1912) was born in Massachusetts. During the Civil War she nursed men on battlefields. In 1881 she formed the American Red Cross.

Winslow Homer (1836-1910) was born in Boston. He became an artist. He is known for his pictures of the sea. Artist James Abbott McNeill Whistler (1834-1903) was born in Lowell. He painted the very famous picture usually called *Whistler's Mother*.

Many inventors and scientists have lived in the Bay State. Eli Whitney (1765-1825) was born in Westborough (WEHST • burr • oh). He invented the cotton gin. Samuel Morse was born in Charlestown in 1791. He invented the telegraph. Elias Howe (ee • LYE • uhs HOW) was born in Spencer in 1819. Howe invented the modern sewing machine. Scientist Luther Burbank was born in Lancaster (LANG • kess • tuhr) in 1849. He developed a new kind of potato and other new plants.

Susan B. Anthony (1820-1906) was born in Adams, Massachusetts. She worked for women's right to vote.

Home to presidents John Adams . . . John Quincy Adams . . . and John F. Kennedy.

The place where the Pilgrims landed . . . where the country's first college was founded . . . and where the first shots of the Revolutionary War were fired.

Today an important state for manufacturing and fishing.

This is the Bay State—Massachusetts.

Facts About MASSACHUSETTS

Area—8,257 square miles (45th biggest state).

Greatest Distance North to South—110 miles

Greatest Distance East to West—190 miles

Borders—The states of Vermont and New Hampshire to the north; the Atlantic Ocean to the east; the Atlantic Ocean and the states of Rhode Island and Connecticut to the south; the state of New York to the west

Highest Point—3,491 feet above sea level (Mount Greylock)

Lowest Point—Sea level, along the Atlantic Ocean

Hottest Recorded Temperature—107°F. (at Chester and New Bedford, on August 2, 1975)

Coldest Recorded Temperature—Minus 34°F. (at Birch Hill Dam, on January 18, 1957)

Statehood—Our sixth state, on February 6, 1788

Origin of Name Massachusetts—Massachusetts was named for the Massachusett Indian tribe; the name is thought to mean "the place of the great hill"

Capital—Boston

Counties—14

U.S. Senators—2

U.S. Representatives—11

State Senators—40

State Representatives—160

State Song—"All Hail to Massachusetts," by Arthur J. Marsh

State Motto—*Ense petit placidam sub libertate quietem* (Latin meaning "By the sword we seek peace, but peace only under liberty")

Main Nickname—The Bay State

Other Nicknames—The Old Bay State, the Old Colony State, the Puritan State, the Baked Bean State

State Seal—Adopted in 1780; revised version adopted in 1898

State Flag—Adopted in 1908

State Flower—Mayflower

State Bird—Chickadee

State Tree—American elm

State Horse—Morgan horse

State Dog—Boston Terrier

State Fish—Cod

State Insect—Ladybug

State Beverage—Cranberry juice

State Fossil—Dinosaur track

State Colors—Blue and gold

Main River—Connecticut River

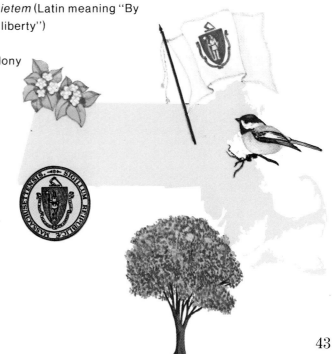

43

Some Other Rivers—Blackstone, Charles, Chicopee, Deerfield, Millers, Westfield, Farmington, Hoosic, Housatonic, Merrimack, Concord

Lakes and Ponds—More than 1,100

National Parklands—10

State Parks—42

Animals—Deer, foxes, porcupines, skunks, rabbits, muskrats, pheasants, ducks, geese, sea gulls, herons, many other kinds of birds, rattlesnakes and other snakes

Fishing—Sea scallops, cod, flounder, tuna, clams, lobsters, swordfish, sea herring, tarpon

Farm Products—Milk, flowers and other plants grown in greenhouses and nurseries, eggs, turkeys, beef cattle, hogs, sheep, cranberries, tomatoes, strawberries, corn, apples, potatoes, tobacco

Mining—Clay, marble, sand, gravel, quartz, granite, limestone

Manufacturing Products—Machinery, television parts and other electric equipment, scientific instruments, metal products, books and other printed products, many kinds of packaged foods, chemicals, paper and paper products

Population—5,737,037 (1980 census)

Major Cities—Boston   562,994 (1980 census)
          Springfield   152,319
          Worcester   161,799
          Cambridge   95,322
          Fall River   92,574
          New Bedford   98,478
          Brockton   95,172
          Quincy   84,743

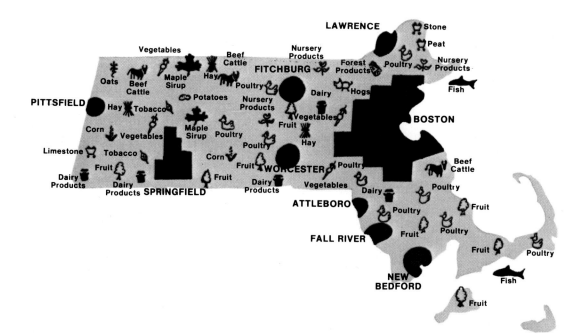

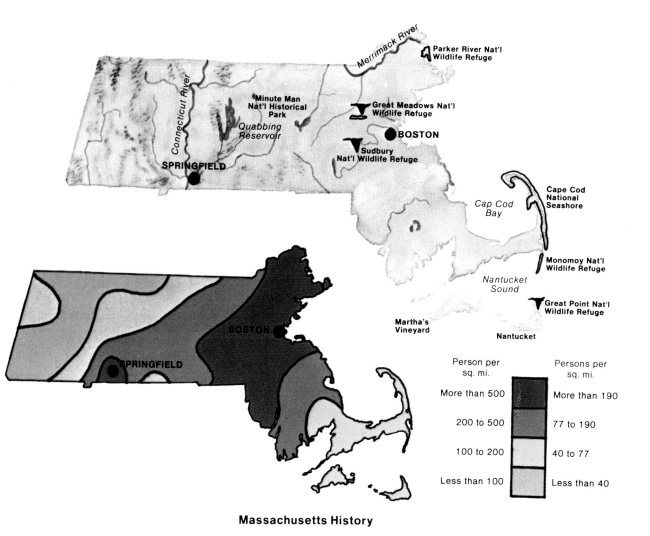

Massachusetts History

There were people in Massachusetts at least 10,000 years ago.

1000—In about this year, Norsemen led by Leif Ericson may have explored Massachusetts

1498—In this year, John Cabot may have explored Massachusetts for England

1602—Bartholomew Gosnold explores Massachusetts for England

1620—The Pilgrims arrive at Plymouth

1621—The Pilgrims celebrate our first Thanksgiving

1630—Boston is founded

1635—The Boston Latin School, the first public school in what is now the United States, is founded

1636—Harvard, the first college in what is now the United States, is founded

1638—The first library in the colonies is established at Harvard

1675-1678—The settlers win "King Philip's War"

1689-1763—Colonists join the British to win the French and Indian Wars

1690—First newspaper in the colonies is printed in Boston (and has only one issue)

1691—The Plymouth Colony and the Massachusetts Bay Colony unite to form
        one Massachusets colony that is ruled by England

1704—The *Boston News-Letter,* the first successful newspaper in America, is
        founded

1763—French and Indian War ends, with England winning; to pay for the war,
        England then places heavy taxes on the American colonists

1770—In the Boston Massacre, English soldiers kill five Americans

1773—The Boston Tea Party brings the American colonies and England
        closer to war

1775—On April 19, the Revolutionary War begins at Lexington and Concord;
        on June 17 the Americans lose the Battle of Bunker Hill

1776—In the first big American victory of the Revolutionary War, the
        Americans drive the English out of Boston

1783—About 88,000 Massachusetts men have helped the United States win
        the Revolutionary War

1788—Massachusetts becomes our sixth state on February 6; Boston is the
        capital

1797—John Adams, born in Quincy, Massachusetts, becomes the second
        president of the United States

1800—Population of Massachusetts is 422,845

1825—John Quincy Adams becomes our sixth president

1831—William Lloyd Garrison begins to publish the antislavery newspaper
        The *Liberator* in Boston

1832—New England Anti-Slavery Society is formed in Boston

1861-1865—During the Civil War, about 160,000 Massachusetts men help
        the North win

1876—Alexander Graham Bell invents the telephone in Boston

1891—James A. Naismith of Springfield invents basketball

1897—The first subway train in the United States opens at Boston

1900—Population of the Bay State reaches 2,805,346

1912—After textile (cloth) workers strike at Lawrence, conditions are
        improved in United States textile factories

1917-1918—After the United States enters World War I, about 198,000
        Massachusetts people are in uniform

1923—Calvin Coolidge (born in Vermont but a governor of Massachusetts)
        becomes the 30th President

1928—First computer developed by Dr. Vannevar Bush of the Massachusetts
        Institute of Technology in Cambridge

1938—Hurricane hits state, killing hundreds

1941-1945—After the United States enters World War II, about 556,000
        Massachusetts men and women serve

1942—A big fire in Boston kills almost 500 people

1961—John Fitzgerald Kennedy, born in Brookline, Massachusetts, becomes
        our 35th President

1971—Program begins to reorganize state government

1980—Boston celebrates its 350th birthday

1983—Michael S. Dukakis begins four-year term as Governor

INDEX

47

INDEX, Cont'd

About the Author:

Dennis Fradin attended Northwestern University on a creative writing scholarship and graduated in 1967. While still at Northwestern, he published his first stories in *Ingenue* magazine and also won a prize in *Seventeen's* short story competition. A prolific writer, Dennis Fradin has been regularly publishing stories in such diverse places as *The Saturday Evening Post, Scholastic, National Humane Review, Midwest,* and *The Teaching Paper.* He has also scripted several educational films. Since 1970 he has taught second grade reading in a Chicago school—a rewarding job, which, the author says, "provides a captive audience on whom I test my children's stories." Married and the father of three children, Dennis Fradin spends his free time with his family or playing a myriad of sports and games with his childhood chums.

About the Artists:

Len Meents studied painting and drawing at Southern Illinois University and after graduation in 1969 he moved to Chicago. Mr. Meents works full time as a painter and illustrator. He and his wife and child currently make their home in LaGrange, Illinois.

Richard Wahl, graduate of the Art Center College of Design in Los Angeles, has illustrated a number of magazine articles and booklets. He is a skilled artist and photographer who advocates realistic interpretations of his subjects. He lives with his wife and two sons in Libertyville, Illinois.